Small Billy and the Midnight Star

Written by Nette Hilton

Illustrated by Bruce Whatley

Hodder
Children's
Books

A division of Hachette Children's Books

A bilby is a small, endangered Australian animal, about the size of a cat.
It lives in a burrow and mostly comes out at night.

This book is dedicated to **Rose-Marie Dusting**,
the recognised creator of the concept of the Easter Bilby.

Bruce Whatley used pen and ink wash on watercolour paper
for the illustrations in this book

First published 2006 by Working Title Press, Adelaide, Australia

This edition published in 2007
by Hodder Children's Books
338 Euston Road, London, NW1 3BH

Type set in Caslon by Patricia Howes
Printed in China

A catalogue record of this book is available from the British Library.

HB ISBN 9780340944493
PB ISBN 9780340944509

10 9 8 7 6 5 4 3 2 1

Hodder Children's Books is a division of Hachette Children's Books.

For more information on bilbies, take a look at: www.wpsa.org.au

Every night, Small Billy, the smallest bilby in the bilby patch sat under the midnight sky to watch the stars.

*H*e loved them all. Every single one
of them.

But the one he loved best was the smallest
one, which hung close to the edge of
the sky.

Every night he reached up to her. And she
shone down on him.

But she was so very far away.

"Sometimes I'm scared that she won't be there," Small Billy said after a long hard bilby-busy day.

He stretched his arms out wide and called, "I love you, star! I love you best of all!"

The star shone down. An especially bright shine.

"See," said the oldest bilby in the bilby patch. "She loves you, too."

And for a little while, from the time it took the moon to wander from the low side of the hill to the high side of the hill, Small Billy felt better.

But when a passing cloud hid the star from view, he grew frightened all over again.

"What if she goes away and forgets me and never, ever comes back?" he said.

"She'll be there," said the oldest bilby. "She always comes back."

The star hurried out from behind the cloud and beamed down on him, splashing his whiskers with starlight and brushing his ears with silver.

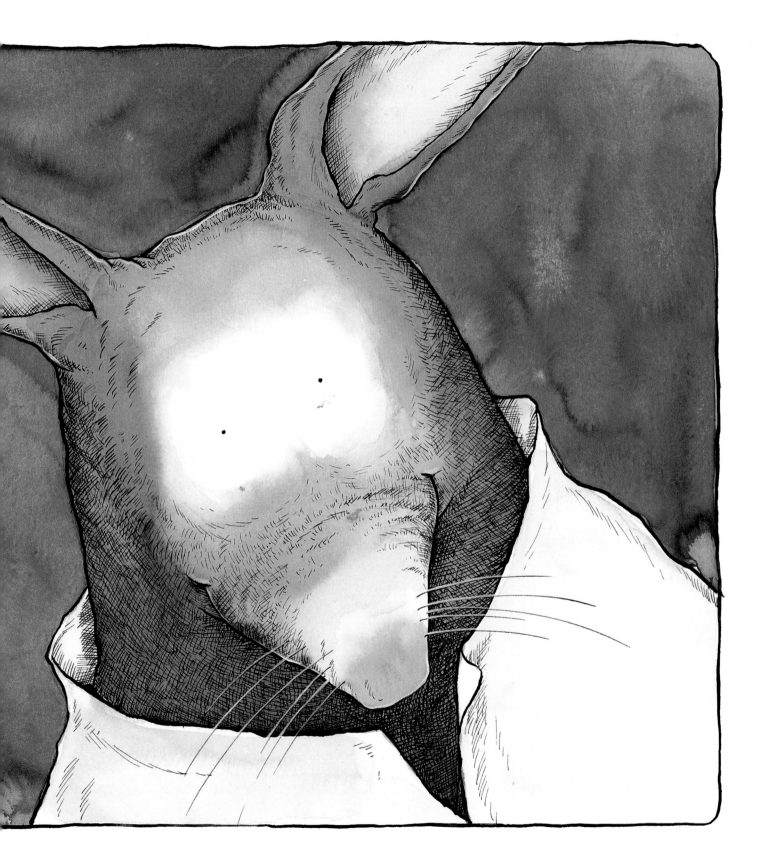

But Small Billy could only think of the midnight sky without his star.

"I need to give her something!" he said. "Something to make her remember me, forever and always."

"I know!" he called out to the star. "I'll give you a kiss!"

He stretched up on tiptoe and tried to kiss her. But he just wasn't tall enough.

"*W*as that a kiss?" asked one of the
little bilbies.

"Not yet," said Small Billy, "but it
soon will be!"

He stood on a rock on the top of the hill
and opened his arms wide and reached up
high. But he still couldn't reach.

*S*o he set off to fetch another rock. And then another.

The star shone down, leading Small Billy from one star-shiny rock to the next.

"What are you doing?" asked the oldest bilby.

"We know," said the little ones. "He's building a kiss."

"You can't build a kiss!" said the oldest bilby with a smile.

"He can! He can!" sang the little ones. "And so can we!"

One by one, two by two, three by three, the little bilbies of the bilby patch joined in, fetching and carrying, lifting and pushing each star-shiny rock all the way to the top of the hill.

And high above them the star shone down from the fading night sky.

Little by little, rock by rock, the kiss grew
higher and bigger and rounder and fatter
until it almost, almost touched the sky.

"Are we there yet?" asked the little bilbies.
"Are we? Are we?"

"Almost," said Small Billy.

"That's not a kiss!" said the oldest bilby
in the bilby patch.

"No," said Small Billy as he climbed from
one star-dappled rock to another.

"This is a kiss."

And, opening his arms wide enough
to hold the whole heavens, he reached up
on tip-tiptoe and kissed the smallest star
at the edge of the dawn sky.

All the bilbies in the bilby patch caught their breath. Not a whisker or a nose twitched.

The little star grew bigger and bigger and brighter and brighter until the desert glowed with the colours of the morning sky, and the rocks on top of the hill blazed gold and purple and crimson.

She sparkled on the pools in the river bed until they flashed like glass beads.

She dusted the tops of the spinifex with copper.

She danced above the little bilbies in the bilby patch and tickled their tummies with star shine.

And then she shone her deepest, clearest light right onto the smallest bilby of all.

"Look at that," said the little bilbies.

"She won't forget you now," whispered the oldest bilby in the bilby patch.

"And I'll remember her," said Small Billy. "Forever … and always."